THREE
GOLD
PIECES

For my father and my mother

THREE
GOLD
PIECES

A Greek Folk Tale retold and illustrated by

ALIKI

Pantheon Books

189266

Once upon a time in a Greek village, there lived a very poor man named Yannis. Although he worked from morning until night, Yannis could barely earn enough to buy his wife and son their daily bread.

One day Yannis decided that if he wanted to make a better life for his family, he had to go abroad, where jobs were better.

He told his family he must leave them, but promised to return when he had earned enough to buy them the things they needed.

The following day, Yannis set off on his long trip.

For three weeks he walked until at last he reached the bustling city of Constantinople.

But though he searched for days, Yannis could find no job. There were many others like him who wanted work.

At last he heard that a wealthy old man needed a servant. Yannis hastened to see him.

The old man liked Yannis and hired him at once.

Yannis became a faithful servant. He was given his lodging and food, but his master kept his pay. He said he would give it to Yannis someday, in one large sum.

Yannis knew that even this was better than his job in the village, so he was satisfied.

Ten years passed. Yannis missed his family very much, and decided to return to them. He told the old man his plans.

"You have been a good servant, Yannis," he said. "Here is the money you have earned—three gold pieces." With that, he bid Yannis goodbye.

Yannis could not believe his eyes. So little money for ten years' toil! But since he could do nothing, he took the coins and said goodbye.

Just as he was leaving, the old man called him back.

"Give me a gold piece, Yannis, and I will give you a good piece of advice."

Although Yannis wanted to refuse, he obediently returned one coin.

"Remember," said his employer. *"Never ask about something that is not your concern."*

"Very well, Master," said Yannis.

He started to leave again when the old man called him a second time.

"Give me another coin, and I will give you another bit of advice."

At this, Yannis hesitated, wondering how he could return home with only one piece of gold.

However, he reluctantly gave the coin to his master, who said, *"Never leave a path you have taken!"*

Yannis promised, and started off once more. But again he heard his name.

"Yannis, give me your last gold piece and I will give you another piece of advice."

For the third time, the poor man could not refuse.

"Remember this," said his employer. "*Suppress your evening anger until morning.*"

"Very well, Master," replied Yannis. And he left the house with nothing to show for all those years but a furrowed brow.

After he had walked for a time, Yannis came to a huge tree. High on a branch sat a Moor sticking gold pieces to the leaves. Yannis thought it was a curious sight, but he remembered his master's advice, and continued on his way.

As soon as he had passed, the Moor called him back.

"For a hundred and seven years I have been sticking gold pieces to these leaves," he said. "Of all the people who passed, you are the very first who did not stop to ask me why."

"It was not my concern," Yannis replied.

The Moor was pleased and said, "Your good sense deserves a reward."

He shook the tree, and gold fell like moonbeams.

"Take these coins, my friend. I am sure you will be able to use them."

Delighted by such good fortune, Yannis stuffed his pockets and his bundle with all the gold he could carry. Then he thanked the Moor and went off, thinking what good advice his master had given him.

A few days later, Yannis saw a long line of mules led by three men. Since they were travelling in the same direction, he asked if he might sit on a mule to rest.

"Of course," said one of the drivers. "They are burdened as it is. One more load won't matter."

So Yannis sat, and together they went on.

Soon they came to an inn, and the hungry drivers decided to stop. They asked Yannis to join them. But he remembered the second piece of advice, and did not want to leave the path he had taken.

"I'll stay here and mind your mules," he said, and settled down to wait.

But as soon as the men had gone through the door,
the ground shook violently and the inn collapsed.
Everyone was buried inside.

Thankful that he had heeded his master's advice, Yannis took the abandoned mules and proceeded on his journey.

Three nights later, Yannis finally reached his village. Happily he gazed at the familiar roads and houses. And when he knocked on his own door, his joy leapt within him.

In a moment it opened, and there stood his wife. He saw at once that she did not recognize him, and decided not to tell her right away.

"I am sorry to trouble you so late," he said. "But I wonder if my mules and I may rest here for the night."

"I cannot ask you into my house," answered the woman kindly. "But there in the yard is a shed where you may rest."

Yannis smiled to himself as he tied the animals, thinking of her surprise when she'd recognize him.

Suddenly he saw a man enter the house. His joy turned to rage.

"So," he thought, "my wife tired of waiting, and took another husband."

He grabbed his musket and started toward the door. Then he remembered the third piece of advice, and decided to wait until morning.

All night Yannis lay awake. At daybreak he rose before the cock crowed, and went out to feed the mules. Sounds from the house told him his wife, too, was up.

Suddenly the door flew open. There stood the man he had seen the night before.

"I am going now, Mother dear," he called. "I will send you some beans for lunch."

Yannis gasped. It was his own son, grown to manhood, whom he had nearly harmed. He ran to embrace the young man, and explained who he was.

Then together they rushed into the house, where the joyful family was reunited.

Later, when his story was told, Yannis opened the bundle of gold and unloaded the mules. There they found enough to keep them content for the rest of their lives.